R

D1103398

Library Services
Victoria Buildings
Queen Street
Falkirk
FK2 7AF

REA
F
VRB

Falkirk Council

First published in the United Kingdom in 2005
by Chrysalis Children's Books,
an imprint of Chrysalis Books Group plc
The Chrysalis Building
Bramley Road
London W10 6SP
www.chrysalisbooks.co.uk

This book was created for Chrysalis Children's Books by Zuza Books.
Text and illustrations copyright © Zuza Books

Zuza Vrbova asserts her moral right to be
identified as the author of this work.
Tom Morgan-Jones asserts his moral right to be
identified as the illustrator of this work.

BRITISH LIBRARY CATALOGUING-IN-PUBLICATION DATA
A catalogue record for this book is available from the British Library.

ISBN 1 84458 480 1

Printed in China
2 4 6 8 10 9 7 5 3 1

Roddy

Learns a Lesson

Zuza Vrbova

Illustrated by Tom Morgan-Jones

CHRYSALIS CHILDREN'S BOOKS

Roddy was a bully. He knew what he liked and
he knew what he didn't like. More than anything else,
he liked his football.

"Let's tear up your favourite picture!" he said to Kit one day, as he ripped the picture off the wall. He tore it into tiny pieces.

"Hello, Four-Eyes," he said to Misty because she was wearing glasses.

Then he sat on Ellie's favourite hat so that it was squashed forever.

Roddy thought being horrible to everyone was funny.

And he loved to stomp about and annoy his classmates.

He liked to grab Lauren and Lucy's skipping rope
and tangle it up in the big oak tree. The twins
didn't like this at all.

And he never went anywhere without his beloved football.

Roddy didn't like school. He didn't like having to sit still. And he never paid attention to what Miss Roo said.

Most of the things that Roddy loved to do were never taught at school – things like how to eat faster or how to kick stones or how to throw balls at people.

8

All the really important things are not taught, Roddy thought.

Miss Roo always said, "Roddy! Behave yourself!" in a sharp voice. But Roddy always thought he WAS behaving himself.

One day, during spelling practice, Miss Roo
asked the class, "How do you spell FLY?"

That gives me an idea, thought Roddy.
He tore out the last page of his exercise book
and made a paper aeroplane.

It was a beauty. It had a supersonic shape with a long triangular nose and light wings.

Perfect for target practice, thought Roddy, wondering who his target could be.

Fred was in the middle of writing 'fly' when something hit him right on the nose. It was Roddy's aeroplane. Fred picked it up and threw it back.

Just at that moment, Miss Roo looked up.

"Fred! Stand in the corner for the rest of the lesson!"
she ordered.

"It wasn't me!" wailed Fred.

But it was no use. For the rest of the lesson,
Fred stood in the corner while Roddy grinned
from ear to ear.

At playtime, Fred said, "We've got to do something."

"Absolutely!" Tabby shouted.

"Absolutely!" agreed Leo.

Even shy George thought it was high time.

Ellie didn't say anything. She was still trying to straighten her hat.

"But what shall we do?" asked Connie.

"Let's give him a taste of his own medicine!" said Tabby.

"Stuff him in the broom cupboard!" cried Leo.

"Tie him to the oak tree!" exclaimed Fred.

"Post him to the other side of the world!" shouted Eddie.

"Let's be serious," said Tabby. "I have a plan."

Everyone leaned forward to listen to Tabby's plan.

"Let's hide his football," she whispered.

"But how?" asked Connie. "He's so big and strong!"

"We'll trick him!" said Tabby.

"But HOW?" asked the others.

As usual, Tabby had a plan. "I'll pretend that it's my birthday and I'll bake a cake," she said.

"I'll invite everyone to taste it at a party in the sports hall. Everyone, that is, EXCEPT Roddy. Then he'll be sure to come. While he is eating the cake, we'll snatch his ball and hide it. Then we will make him promise to behave himself before we give it back!" Tabby said grinning.

"Now, let's go to the sports hall. We need to get our plan started," she ordered.

"Ellie, you have the best handwriting. You can write
the invitation," suggested Fred.

Ellie wrote, 'You are invited to Tabby's Birthday Party
in the sports hall.'

Then she drew a huge cake and put the card in an envelope.

"I'll make the cake when I get home and bring it to school tomorrow," said Tabby.

"And when Roddy is busy eating it, I will take the ball and hide it," suggested Eddie bravely.

The next day, Roddy noticed something being passed around the classroom.

"What's that?" He shoved Ellie aside to take a look.

"None of your business," Fred said. But Roddy snatched the envelope from his hand.

This sounds JUST like my business, he thought,

licking his lips. He tried to imagine what

it would be like to eat a WHOLE birthday cake.

At playtime, everyone waited in the sports hall.

Scrunch, scrunch came the sound of
Roddy's feet on the path outside.

"Cake, cake, glorious cake," Roddy was singing
to himself.

When Roddy saw George standing outside
the hall, he shouted, "Get out of my way, Pinhead!"
And he kicked his ball at him.

George ducked out of the way just in time,
and Eddie caught the ball.

But Roddy had forgotten all about his ball –
he had spotted the cake!

Roddy didn't notice his missing ball until he was
halfway through the cake. He charged outside
and saw Eddie hiding it in the big oak tree.

"Give me my ball back, you thieves!"
he yelled. "I'm going to get you for this!"

And he stamped his feet and jumped up
and down in a rage.

"It's your own fault," Tabby said. "We'll give you
your ball back, but first you have to promise
never to do those horrible things again."

"What horrible things?" Roddy asked.

"You threw a paper aeroplane at my nose!" said Fred.

"You sat on my favourite hat," whispered Ellie, hiding behind Eddie.

"Do you promise never to do those things again?" asked Tabby.

"Yes, yes, yes," whimpered Roddy, "I promise.
Just give me my ball back." He tried to pretend
that he wasn't crying.

Tabby gave Roddy his ball back.
"Remember your promise!" she warned.

After school, Roddy walked home with his ball tucked firmly under his arm. He thought about what had happened that day. And he remembered his promise.

If I stop doing horrible things, I might make some friends, he thought. And if I make friends, I'll have someone to play football with!

Top of the Class

Collect them all!

Ellie Takes a Chance
Zuza Vrbova
Illustrated by Tom Morgan-Jones
1-84458-483-6

Zoë Wins the Race
Zuza Vrbova
Illustrated by Tom Morgan-Jones
1-84458-407-0

Piers Finds his Voice
Zuza Vrbova
Illustrated by Tom Morgan-Jones
1-84458-406-2

George Makes Friends
Zuza Vrbova
Illustrated by Tom Morgan-Jones
1-84458-482-8

Tabby Saves the Day
Zuza Vrbova
Illustrated by Tom Morgan-Jones
1-84458-481-X

Kit Paints the Sky
Zuza Vrbova
Illustrated by Tom Morgan-Jones
1-84458-404-6

Leo Takes to the Stage
Zuza Vrbova
Illustrated by Tom Morgan-Jones
1-84458-405-4

Roddy Learns a Lesson
Zuza Vrbova
Illustrated by Tom Morgan-Jones
1-84458-480-1

Visit the Top of the Class website at
www.topoftheclassbooks.com